Playmakers

Pitchers

Lynn M. Stone

Rourke
Publishing LLC
Vero Beach, Florida 32964

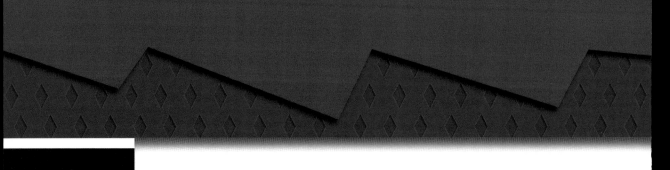

www.rourkepublishing.com

PHOTO CREDITS: All photos © Lynn M. Stone

Editor: Robert Stengard-Olliges

Cover and page design by Tara Raymo

Library of Congress Cataloging-in-Publication Data

Stone, Lynn M.
  Pitchers / Lynn Stone.
      p. cm. -- (Playmakers)
  Includes bibliographical references.
  ISBN 978-1-60044-594-1
  1. Pitching (Baseball)--Juvenile literature. 2. Pitchers (Baseball)--Juvenile literature.
I. Title.
  GV871.S697 2008
  796.357'22--dc22

                                  2007019104

Printed in the USA

CG/CG

Rourke Publishing

www.rourkepublishing.com – rourke@rourkepublishing.com
Post Office Box 3328, Vero Beach, FL 32964

Table of Contents

The Pitcher   4

The Pitcher's Skills   10

So, You Want to Be a Pitcher?   18

Glossary   23

Index   24

The Pitcher

The pitcher is the baseball player who throws the ball to batters of the opposing team. A pitcher's job is to make it difficult for a **batter** to hit the pitched ball, or at least to hit it well. A skilled pitcher is so important that he can sometimes decide the outcome of a baseball game.

A pitcher (left) hurls a baseball to a right-handed batter standing at the plate on a baseball diamond.

A pitch sails into the strike zone where a batter waits to swing.

A pitcher has to throw the ball into a relatively small area, called the **strike zone**. If a pitch does not enter the zone, the batter should not swing at it. Pitches outside the strike zone are called "balls" by the umpire if the batter does not swing. If a batter collects four pitches called balls, he will be awarded first base on a **base on balls**, or walk.

Left foot on the rubber of the mound, a left-handed pitcher throws a baseball toward home plate.

A pitcher throws from an elevated mound to the catcher, crouched behind home plate. The pitcher begins his pitching motion, called a wind-up, with his foot touching a rectangular slab called the **pitching rubber**. The regulation distance from the rubber to home plate in professional baseball is 60 feet, 6 inches (18.4 meters). The Little League distance from rubber to plate is 46 feet (14 meters).

Many pitchers specialize as **starting pitchers** or **relief pitchers**. A "closer" is a relief pitcher who usually pitches just the ninth inning to protect a team's lead.

This Little League pitch looks quick to the batter, but a pitched ball may travel at more than 90 miles (144 kilometers) per hour in baseball's upper levels!

The Pitcher's Skills

A pitcher must have what is often called "a good arm," which basically means that he can throw a ball hard and he can throw it hard repeatedly. Many pitchers throw at least 85 to 100 pitches in a baseball game.

A pitcher begins his "windup" from the mound.

A right-handed pitcher pushes off his left foot to release the ball.

As a pitcher follows through to complete the pitch, he squares around to be in position for any ball that the batter might hit toward him.

Typically, the best pitchers throw a baseball at a high speed and throw it with accuracy. Speed is important, but not all pitchers have the same natural movement on their pitches. In other words, a pitched baseball does not fly from everyone's hand in a straight line. A pitcher with "great movement" on his pitches has a greater chance of fooling a batter, because the ball moves around as it flies.

Still, pitchers without 90 to 95 mile per hour (152-kilometer) fastballs can be successful if they have other skills. The greatest of these is accuracy. A pitcher who can target a baseball into "spots" at the edges of the strike zone can often make up for a lack of velocity with carefully placed pitches. Pitchers who can throw a baseball at different speeds and with a range of movement—such as a sharply-breaking **curve ball**—can also be successful without overpowering **fastballs**.

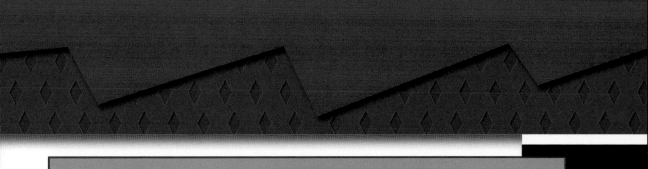

A pitcher's grip on the ball determines which pitch he will throw, such as a fastball, curve, or slider.

In addition to throwing a baseball to a catcher, a pitcher must be able to field his position. The pitcher has to be alert for hard-hit ground balls, line drives, and slow-rolling, **bunted** balls that come his way. A pitcher also has to sometimes cover first base, and he must back up the catcher in certain situations.

Part of a pitcher's job is to keep runners from stealing bases. A left-handed pitcher throws to first base to keep a runner close to the base.

After fielding a ground ball hit to him, a pitcher throws the ball to first base.

So, You Want to Be a Pitcher?

Pitchers may be large or small. Most Major Leaguers are big men, but others stand less than 6 feet (1.8 meters) tall and weigh less than 200 pounds (90 kilograms).

A pitcher peeks over his shoulder at a runner on first base. Pitchers shorten their windup to "the stretch" motion when dealing with most base runners.

The right-handed pitcher here has a natural advantage over the right-handed batter facing him.

Pitchers can be left- or right-handed. Right-handed pitchers have some advantage simply because more batters are right-handers. The natural movement of a pitch from a right-handed pitcher generally makes the ball tail away from a right-handed batter. That makes it more difficult for a right-handed batter to hit well.

When considering pitchers, baseball coaches look for players who can throw a baseball hard and throw it with accuracy. Even a hard-throwing pitcher will not be successful at the upper levels of baseball if he cannot regularly throw into the strike zone.

Successful pitching requires the cooperation of arm, shoulder, and legs.

The catcher catches a strike.

A pitcher has to work closely with his catcher. A good pitcher shows leadership and **composure** on the field. But because of his dependence upon the catcher, he should not be stubborn. A catcher calls many of the pitches that a pitcher throws. That means the catcher often decides where he wants a pitch thrown—such as inside or outside—and what kind of pitch he wants thrown. By the high school level, most successful pitchers have command of at least two pitches, a fastball and a curve ball.

The catcher helps a pitcher choose a pitch, and the catcher's mitt gives the pitcher a target at the plate.

Glossary

base on balls (BAYSS ON BAWLZ) — the automatic awarding of first base to a batter after four pitches called by the umpire outside the strike zone

batter (BAT ur) — the player with a bat who stands at home plate awaiting a pitch

bunted (buhn TED) — hitting a ball soft on purpose

composure (kuhm POH zhur) — calmness and control under pressure

curve ball (KURV BAWL) — a baseball pitched in such a way that it suddenly "breaks," or curves, away from a batter

fastball (FAST BAWL) — a baseball pitched at high speed

pitching rubber (PICH ing RUHB ur) — the rubbery, rectangular slab on a pitching mound; the point at which a pitcher must begin his pitch to the plate

relief pitcher (ri LEEF PICH ur) — any pitcher who comes into a game to replace a starting pitcher

starting pitcher (STAR ting PICH ur) — a pitcher who starts a game and is expected to pitch several innings

strike zone (STRIKE ZOHN) — the area over home plate into which a pitch must go if it is to be called a strike by the home plate umpire

Index

accuracy   13, 20

curve ball   14, 22

fastball   14, 22

first base   5, 16

home plate   7

mound   7

strike zone   5, 14, 20

team   4, 8

umpire   5

Further Reading

Gigliotti, Jim. *Power Pitchers*. Child's World, 2007.

Gigliotti, Jim. *1,001 Facts about Pitchers*. DK Publishing, 2004.

Oster, Don. *Guide for Young Softball Pitchers*. Lyons Press, 2005.

Website to Visit

http://www.baseball-reference.com/bullpen/Pitcher

http://www.everything2.com/index.pl?node=pitcher

About the Author

Lynn M. Stone is the author of more than 400 children's books. He is a talented natural history photographer as well. Lynn, a former teacher, travels worldwide to photograph wildlife in its natural habitat.